Praise for
GARY PAULSEN'S
The Cookcamp

"A beautifully written book of a boy's healing trust in people."
—*Horn Book Guide*

"This is vintage Paulsen—the harsh, northern, isolated setting, the survival theme, universal truths simply stated, and powerful description." —*Booklist*

"In its simplicity of story line but depth of imagery and emotion, Paulsen's latest work is very much like MacLachlan's *Sarah, Plain and Tall*. . . . While the boy is very young, his experiences are universal, making this a superb book for readers just old enough to look back and remember their childhoods and grandparents with a feeling of nostalgia."
—*School Library Journal*

This short, lyrical novel . . . strikes extraordinary emotional chords . . . Paulsen expertly balances sensitive probing of the boy's mental and emotional life with superb descriptions of the boy helping the men build the road, making Paulsen's unnamed hero one of the most fully realized characters in recent memory. Those hungry for adventure stories, as well as more introspective readers, will be spellbound by this stirring novel, which is every bit the equal of *The Winter Room* and Paulsen's other works."
—*Publishers Weekly*

APPLE SIGNATURE EDITIONS

The Classroom at the End of the Hall
by Douglas Evans

Afternoon of the Elves
by Janet Lisle Taylor

Somewhere in the Darkness
by Walter Dean Myers

Bad Girls
by Cynthia Voigt

The Fire Pony
by Rodman Philbrick

The Music of Dolphins
by Karen Hesse

Faith and the Electric Dogs
by Patrick Jennings

THE
COOKCAMP

THE
COOKCAMP

GARY PAULSEN

SCHOLASTIC 📖 SIGNATURE
AN IMPRINT OF SCHOLASTIC INC.

New York Toronto London Auckland Sydney
Mexico City New Delhi Hong Kong Buenôs Aires

ISBN 0-439-52357-5

12 11 10 9 8 7   5 6 7 8/0

Printed in the U.S.A.   40

First Scholastic trade paperback printing, June 2003

To the memory of
MY GRANDMOTHER

THE
COOKCAMP

PROLOGUE

For a long time during a war his father was in the army and had to be away to fight, and the boy had to go live with his grandmother.

Of course, nothing happens that smoothly. Going to live with his grandmother did not come about so easily.

His mother had taken a job in a factory because she said they needed the money.

The boy was only five years old, but even then he knew they did not need the money. Checks came each month from the army, and another came from his grandfather—his father's father—so they did not need the money.

It was that his mother was bored. She was bored and did not want to spend endless days sitting in the apartment listening to the radio and drinking coffee and waiting.

The boy knew—sensed—that. He had heard her say it.

He felt the same.

He tried to tell her so, his mother, tried to tell her he felt the same, but she didn't hear it in some way, and she took a job in a factory and he was sent to live with his grandmother.

Still it did not happen that smoothly.

At first his mother hired a baby-sitter and kept him in the apartment.

But the baby-sitter was a crazy woman who sat and drank red wine and listened to and talked to the radio soap operas all day and didn't bathe and smelled bad, and so he was sent to live with his grandmother in the north.

But even then what happened was not to be as gentle and smooth as that.

He learned to be around the baby-sitter and to live with her so his mother did not know how bad it was, and when she asked if he liked the baby-sitter he shrugged and said:

"Sometimes she makes me hot cereal." He did not add that the hot cereal was Shredded Wheat with hot water from the faucet poured over it and did not say how he had to drain it himself and find a spoon himself or that the cereal came only in the afternoon when he was hungry and whined.

So his mother was fooled, and he could have stayed with her and not gone to be with his grandmother in the north woods.

Except for the man.

The man was tall and had blond hair like his mother's only much shorter. He had a thick neck and full shoulders and a wide smile with large white teeth, and his name was Casey.

Casey came home from the factory with his mother one night.

"You must say hello to Casey," his mother said. "He is your uncle and is going to stay with us for a while."

But of course he was not an uncle at all, and that first night the boy came out of the bedroom in their small apartment and saw his mother with Casey on the couch making sounds he did not understand but did not like—sounds he did not understand but that made him want to not like Casey forever and ever.

And his mother saw him staring at them on the couch.

She pushed Casey away.

She held the boy and cried.

And the next day she pinned a note to his jacket and put him on a train, and he rode alone a day and a night sleeping in a Pullman berth and part of another day to get to the small town by the Canadian border where he would meet his grandmother, who was working as a cook for a rough crew of men building a road up into Canada.

And that was the way it finally happened.

ONE

E HAD never ridden alone on the train before. His mother had been with him the first time, to Chicago, but now the train seemed so different it was like a new world.

The porter read the note pinned to his jacket and put him in a seat at the front of the car. Twice when he had to go to the bathroom the porter took him by the hand and brought him back to the seat when he was finished.

Always smiling, the porter made him relax. The porter brought him comic books. The boy could not read, but the pictures held him for a long part of the ride.

In the middle of the day the porter brought him a lunch in a box and sat with him speaking in low murmurs while the boy ate.

As it started to get dark the porter lowered the bed for the boy and tucked him in. When he tried to stay awake in the compartment and look at comic books, the porter came back.

"Boy needs his sleep," the porter said, and turned the light out. "Boy needs to get his rest. . . ."

And when the boy still couldn't sleep the porter came back again and sat on the edge of his bunk and sang him a long song about a woman in New Orleans.

The song didn't mean much to the boy. It was all about a beautiful woman and a man who broke her heart.

But the words didn't seem to matter. The porter's voice was low and soothing.

> "Ole Josie,
>   laid me low,
>   laid me low.

Ole Josie
took my money
and laid me low. . . ."

The boy lay back in the Pullman bunk and let the porter's music take him down until his eyes closed and he went to sleep thinking only a little about his mother and Casey.

IN THE NIGHT they went through Minneapolis, where the boy had to change trains. The porter bundled him from one train to the next wrapped in a blanket, and he did not really awaken except to half-hear the hiss of steam and sounds of people running in the depot.

In the morning he awakened to the rumble of wheels and opened the curtain on the side of his bed to look outside.

The train was rolling through thick forest— trees that were so richly green and tall and thick it seemed the train was roaring through a green tunnel.

There was not a dining car on the train. After the new porter raised the bunk and dropped the seats into place, he brought the boy a paper bag. Inside was a small bottle of milk, some grapes, and a biscuit with grape jelly, wrapped in waxed paper.

The boy sat up in the seat with the note still pinned to his jacket and ate the grapes and biscuit. The biscuit was crumbly but very good, and when he'd finished each and every crumb he drank the small bottle of milk.

And all this time the train roared through the trees and past lakes and finally, late in the afternoon, it began to slow.

The boy had become bored by the endless green and had dozed off, his face leaning against the glass. The stopping of the train awakened him, and he sat up just as the porter came to his seat.

"This is where you get off," the porter said, smiling. "Your people should be waiting for you in the depot. Make sure you've got all your fixings and come on. . . ."

The boy jumped up and grabbed the sack with his clothes, and the porter took his small suitcase, and he followed the porter out of the car.

Outside it was hot, and the damp heat hit the boy as he came into the opening between the cars. The conductor was standing below on the wooden platform and helped him down.

The first thing he saw was the station. There was no town. The trees had been cleared back, and a single yellow building had been put next to the tracks as a depot. On the side of the building was a sign:

PINE, MINN.

But there was no town, only the one building. The locomotive made hissing and cracking sounds as if impatient to be going, and the boy moved away from the car, afraid of the loud noise and the big steel driver wheels on the engine.

He could not see his grandmother. The depot agent came onto the platform with a canvas mailbag and nodded to the boy, who was standing next to the porter.

"Isn't the boy's family here?" the porter asked.

"Nope." The agent shook his head. "And no word, either, about a boy. . . ."

"Well, we can't take him back on the train." The porter leaned over the platform and spit tobacco juice neatly down by the train wheels.

"We're going up into Canada, sonny, and won't be back until day after tomorrow."

The depot agent rubbed his neck and shook his head. "I don't know. I've just got a cot in the back room—I'm only here two nights." He looked at the boy. "What's your family's name?"

The boy told him the name of his grandmother.

"Halverson," the station agent repeated the name. "Anita Halverson." He shook his head again. "Nope. I don't know the name. . . ."

The whistle on the locomotive gave a sudden blast, and the porter stepped forward. "We're cutting into our running time. I've got an idea. You take him and keep him. If nobody comes for him we'll pick him up on the way back and I'll put you in for two days extra pay."

"Done." The agent nodded, but the porter had already mounted the steps and waved to the engineer. The locomotive snorted and jerked and the train was moving. In minutes the caboose had disappeared around a curve.

In the sudden silence the boy heard a bird singing.

"What's your name, boy?" the agent asked.

The boy told him, but the agent had turned away and didn't hear the answer. He moved into the depot, and after a minute the boy picked up his sack and suitcase and lugged them after the man, trying not to cry.

Inside the depot it was dark and cool. The agent moved into a small room at the end of the building. The boy went to a bench along the wall and sat down with his sack and suitcase next to his feet.

TWO

THE boy sat on the bench and saw all the things there were to see in the depot room. There was a monster stove in one corner for heat in the winter, with a wood-box, scarred and beaten, in back of it where the agent kept wood. It was empty now.

The bench was too high and the boy's feet did not reach the floor and were uncomfortable, felt pinched. He swung them back and forth to loosen them up and thought of how it would be if his grandmother did not come for him.

What would they do?

Send him back to Chicago where his mother worked in the war plant and lived with Uncle Casey and he would have to live with Uncle Casey, probably, though he hated Uncle Casey for the sounds.

There was a clock on the wall with a brass pendulum that swung back and forth, and he watched it, listened to the loud ticking that seemed to fill the whole room. Now and then the agent would move something in the back room, and the boy would hear a thump or a scrape.

Probably they would send him back to Chicago to live if his grandmother didn't come, and when he thought that, he missed his mother and could not keep from crying. He bit his lower lip and kept very quiet, but the tears came just the same and dripped off his cheek down onto his hand while he stared at the clock and thought that it wouldn't even be bad to live with Uncle Casey if his grandmother didn't come and he had to go back to Chicago.

It would be better than sitting on the bench in this old depot where his feet didn't reach the floor, listening to a dumb old clock tick back and forth.

"I'm sure they'll come for you," the agent said, appearing suddenly from the back room. "Your people, I mean. They'll come. Don't worry. Here, take this."

In his hand he held a doughnut that had been dipped in sugar. The boy nodded and thanked him and took the doughnut and bit into it. He was not hungry—had just eaten on the train—but the doughnut tasted good anyway and he ate it all.

"I'd give you something to drink, but I've only got coffee in my thermos and you look a bit young for coffee. . . ."

And he was gone, back into the small room, closing the door behind him and leaving the boy sitting on the bench with the doughnut crumbs on his shirt.

The day passed. No other trains came by, and after what seemed like years sitting on the bench memorizing everything in the room the boy slid down to his feet and went outside on the platform.

Once outside he could hear the sounds of the birds again. A large blue one—he did not know the different kinds of birds—landed on a limb not far from him and made an ugly, squawking sound, then flew to a limb farther down the track.

The boy followed the bird, kept following as it flew slightly farther on until he looked around and was surprised to find that he could not see the depot.

The woods seemed to swoop in on him from both sides of the tracks. Thick and green and closing on him, frightening, and he turned and ran back down the tracks until he came around the curve and saw the depot.

He kept trotting until he was at the platform again, where he sat down in the shade of the building. A mosquito landed on his hand and began to drink and he watched it fill, then squashed it.

"Dumb bug. . . ."

Just then he heard the sound of a motor coming, and he walked around the side of the depot to the back where it met the woods.

A narrow road had been cut through the forest, little more than twin ruts, and as he watched the opening of the road the motor sounds grew louder and still louder until it seemed as if a locomotive would somehow appear in the dirt ruts.

When he thought he'd have to cover his ears, an enormous dump truck suddenly exploded out of the forest on the road and screeched to a halt barely a foot from the wall of the depot in a cloud of dust, scattering gravel.

For a moment the boy could see nothing but dust, but when it began to settle he saw the door on the passenger side of the truck open and a small figure step down, first to the running board, then, hanging on to the handle, down to the ground.

It was his grandmother.

He stood for a second, still in shock from the size and speed of the truck suddenly blasting out of the trees. Then it all caught up with him, the long train ride and Uncle Casey and finding himself alone at the depot, alone in the world with nothing but a sugar doughnut, and he ran to her—ran into her head-on, crying and not caring that he was crying.

"Oh my," she said, wrapping her arms around his head and shoulders and hugging him. "Oh my, look what we found at the depot."

She held him away and used the edge of her

thumb to wipe his eyes. "Did you think we weren't coming for you?"

He nodded, still sniffling.

"Ever and ever not coming for you?"

Again he nodded, but he could see the smile in her eyes and on her face and he smiled as well.

"The truck. Something didn't work right in the truck and we had to stop at many streams and add water to the radiator in the front of it. Many streams."

While she was talking, the door on the driver's side opened and a man seemingly as large as the truck stepped down. He spit off to the side and wiped his chin with his hand—a hand as big as a ham—and snorted: "Fan belt slips. Got to tighten her. She gets hot."

The depot door opened and the agent stepped out, drawn by the sound of the truck motor. He nodded to the driver. "You must be the boy's family."

"Not me. I'm Carl." The big man pointed with his chin. "She's the boy's grandma. I brought her." His words were short, the sentences almost cut off. "We're late. You got a crescent wrench?"

They moved inside, and the boy looked up at his grandmother. "I came alone on the train and they gave me a lunch in a sack with some grapes and we saw miles and miles of trees and more trees. . . ."

She laughed. "And you're going to see a lot more. We're eighty miles by dirt road to where we'll be and it's all woods. All the way."

While she talked her hands moved through his hair, combing it over to the side in gentle strokes. Her hand felt good to him. He leaned against her, smelling the road dust and the exhaust fumes from the truck in her dress.

The agent and the driver came back out and lifted the hood on the truck. They had several wrenches, and after some hammering and swearing they grunted, spit in the dirt, and closed the hood.

"She's tight now, by God," Carl said. Then, when he saw the boy standing close and the look in his grandmother's eyes, he added, "Sorry."

Carl climbed into the truck and waited while the boy and his grandmother went around and climbed up into the seat.

The boy sat in the middle, and he had to sit

with his legs spread apart so Carl could shift the transmission levers on the floor.

Carl started the truck with great coughing sounds and clouds of smoke and went backwards and forwards until the truck was turned around, then started off down the narrow road through the woods.

It was so noisy in the cab that the boy could not hear himself think. Yet Carl kept up a stream of short sentences, punctuating them by spitting snoose out the open window at the side.

"Making a road up into Canada. Something to do with the war. We're too old to be soldiers, but we can build roads. In case the Germans [he said "Chermans"] come over here. We might have to move north. In a hurry."

He yelled so loudly into the boy's ear, leaning down with each sentence, that the boy kept jumping sideways, half-deafened.

"Dumb idea. The road. Starts nowhere and ends nowhere. Just moves through the woods."

Soon the boy was used to even the loud noises, the smoke and whine of the truck grinding along, and he leaned against his grandmother. He felt her warmth through the sleeve of her dress, and even in the summer heat it made him feel good.

But then everything rolled over him. The train ride and the waiting and the bouncing and grinding of the truck over the road and the warmth of his grandmother all came down on him and his eyes closed and he slept again, though this time in peace.

THREE

THE silence awakened him.

Suddenly it was very quiet, and he opened his eyes to find that the truck had stopped. The night was pitch dark and he could see nothing.

"We're home," Carl whispered to him. Large hands wrapped around him under his armpits and lifted him past the steering wheel and down, and Carl carried him through the dark—so black the boy could see nothing—then up some steps and into a small building of some kind.

"I'll light a lamp," his grandmother said. There were some scraping sounds and a splash of yellow light as she struck a match and lit an oil lamp on a table along the wall.

In the glow, the boy could see they were in a long, narrow room with tables and chairs, and benches down the side. At the end was a wood cooking stove and kitchen where the boy could see bins of flour and potatoes. Next to the stove was a small bed and off to the side was a bunk. Carl put the boy on the bunk.

"He's still asleep," Carl said. "Button cute. Like a puppy." But the boy wasn't asleep and heard it.

Carl turned to leave, and the boy's grandmother undressed him and tucked him in. The sheets on the small bed smelled of flowers to the boy, flowers and soft summer smells that he remembered without knowing how he remembered them.

His grandmother went to one of the tables and sat and carefully took the pins out of her hair, which fell in long coils of rich black and gray that hung down her back, and he wanted to see more, wanted to watch her in the yellow light from the lamp but could not.

He could not. No matter the excitement of the day and train ride—no matter.

He could not keep his eyes open, and he was once more asleep.

FOUR

THE noise startled the boy so badly that he jerked up in the small bed and hit his head against the bottom of a shelf overhead.

The noise was deafening—a roar he had never heard before—and for a few seconds he did not know where he was and was frightened, and he cried out.

"What's wrong, little thimble?" His grandmother suddenly appeared and sat on the edge of the bunk. "I'm right here."

"It's the noise—I didn't know where I was. It scared me."

"I'm here," she repeated. "I'll always be here."

She rubbed his forehead and cheeks with the back of her hand, a gentle touch, then used her fingers to straighten his mussed hair. She had her hair back in a bun, gray and black mixed in a thick coiled braid. But some hairs had come loose, and he saw that she had flour on her cheeks.

"What is the noise?" the boy asked, pulling the blanket up around his neck. "It's so loud."

"That's just the men starting the engines on the trucks and the cats. They always run them in the morning before breakfast to loosen the oil. They'll be in to eat soon."

She moved back to the stove, and the boy could feel the heat from it now that he was awake.

He decided he didn't want to be still in bed when the men came in, so he rolled out and put his feet on the floor and stood barefoot in his underwear. He found his pants at the end of the bed and pulled them on and a T-shirt and walked, still barefoot, out around the wood-burning stove.

His grandmother was making biscuits, and she had just finished pulling a pan of them out of the oven on the stove when she saw him.

"I thought you might go back to sleep."

He shook his head but said nothing. The smell from the biscuits seemed to fill the room, fill the world, and when she wiped them with a small cloth smeared with butter so the hot biscuits shone, the smell grew even more powerful. He swallowed again and again, and she smiled and handed him a biscuit split that she'd filled with honey, so hot he almost couldn't hold it, but he ate it and could think of nothing else then.

Just the biscuit and the honey and the butter.

"You can help me," she said when he'd finished the biscuit. "The men will come in soon from the bunk trailer and we have to be ready for them."

She handed him a pile of plates and he went down the tables putting the plates in a row. When he was done she gave him knives and forks and spoons and he placed one of each by the plates, and then cups.

"Put the cups upside down," she said. "The men like to turn them over themselves. That way they know they haven't been used."

"Who would use them?" the boy asked. "Do they think you would use them?"

She shook her head. "It's just a way they are, the men. Just a way they are. Put the cups upside down and you'll see."

He did as she said and then put out salt and pepper shakers made of tin with handles on their sides and cans of condensed milk with holes cut in them for cream pitchers and big tin cans shaped like houses full of syrup, and just then, when he finished putting the syrup on the tables, the engines outside stopped and seconds later the door of the cook trailer slammed open and the men came in.

It was like the outside came in, the boy thought, like the woods came in, like the world came in.

Nine men came through the door to eat, but they were so big, made such big sounds and had such big smells and big clothes, that it seemed like many more. Carl was in first, the one the boy knew, and he spit his snoose into a can by the door and cleaned out his lip with a finger that he wiped on his pants, as did each man after him. They all took their caps off and jammed them in the pockets of their bib overalls. Their hair was mussed and stood every which way, and there was a tight line across each of their foreheads. Below the line their faces were red, dark red to brown, and burned with oil and smoke and sun. Above the line left by their caps their foreheads were a flat, dead white and it made them look surprised all the time.

They sat roughly to the tables, all of them big as houses, the boy thought. They sat to the tables and his grandmother brought heaping platters of pancakes and motioned to the boy to bring the big bowls of biscuits, which he did. Then she brought the huge enamel pot of coffee from the stove and sure enough each man turned his cup over—his hands so big the cup looked like a baby cup—and blew in it and held it up for coffee and she looked at the boy and winked and smiled.

"Yes ma'am," they said to her, and "No ma'am" and "Thank you ma'am," and were so polite the boy almost smiled but didn't. They made him think of big, polite bears.

He had to go for more biscuits. It seemed that as soon as the food was on the table and he'd turned around, it was gone—shoveled in and down somehow without chewing, coffee on top so hot it steamed into their mouths, and talk, always talking and talking.

Laughing. They would tell stories, but before the story was out someone else would tell one over the top of it, and before that was half out another would tell one over the top of the first two, until all of them seemed to be speaking at once and the boy could make no sense of it.

They all ruffled his hair.

They came in like all the outside and ruffled his hair and laughed and talked and ate until everything, everything was gone—all the biscuits and pancakes and coffee—until each and every can of condensed milk had been poured into each and every cup of coffee and was now empty and each sugar bowl was empty and everything was gone. Gone.

Then they rose, almost as one man, rose and put their small-looking, greasy caps on their heads and pinched snoose into their lower lips and said "Thank you, thank you" to the boy's grandmother. "Thank you for the good food."

And outside they stomped, and soon the boy could hear the roar of the engines again. But when he rushed to the small window next to the door he could see nothing but thick forest that came in close to the trailers.

"They're like animals," his grandmother said. "They come in and eat like animals." But he could tell from her voice that she liked them and was proud that her food was eaten by them like animals.

"They're so . . . so big," the boy said. "They aren't like other men." And he was thinking then of Casey who he had thought was big in Chicago but who would have fit under the arms of these men, with room to spare it seemed. He wondered if one of them would beat up on Casey for him if he told them about Casey and his mother and thought maybe Carl would, but he didn't say anything.

His grandmother nodded. "Yes, they are like other men. All men are the same. Even you will be like them one day—just the same. You will grow and you will be the same, even if you are now my little thimble."

AT THE END of the cook trailer there was a tin sink bolted to the wall, and his grandmother took hot water from a bucket on the wood stove and poured it into the sink.

Steam came up around her face and made her hair seem to settle at the sides of her head until it lay damp on her temples and cheeks.

"You bring the dirty dishes to me and we'll wash and get ready for lunch. It comes soon enough."

He went back and forth with plates and cups and silverware, and she washed them about as fast as he brought them, and he only dropped one plate, which didn't even break.

When all the dishes were washed she handed him a damp dish towel. "Wipe all the tables. Just wipe the crumbs to the floor and we'll sweep them out the door."

His arms were not long enough to reach across the tables to wipe. He had to wipe down one side of each and then go around and wipe down the other, and he kept going back and forth that way until all the tables were clean and the crumbs were on the floor. Then his grandmother showed him how to use the cedar broom with the straw bristles to sweep the crumbs outside the door and down the steps onto the ground where a chipmunk came from under a log and ate them.

He had never seen a chipmunk, and he sat

on the steps to watch it while his grandmother went back in the trailer to begin cooking lunch.

The chipmunk ate every crumb that it could find, picking them up and rotating them to smell them on all sides and then nibbling them down with small chewing motions.

The boy put his hand on the step next to a piece of bread, kept very still, and tried to hold his breath as long as he could. And the chipmunk finally came right next to his finger and took the bread. It moved off four or five inches to eat and he thought he would tell his grandmother, but as soon as he moved the chipmunk disappeared. He did not see it leave, did not see it run; one second it was there and the next instant it was gone.

He rose and went into the cook trailer. His grandmother had apples on a table, and spices, and a large crockery bowl in which she was mixing pie-crust dough.

"The chipmunk came right up to my fingers, right next to them, and took a piece of bread."

"I'll bet that if you sat with a bit of dough in your fingers the chipmunk would take it," she said to him, holding out a small lump of dough. "They like pie dough."

"They do?"

"They like everything you like—don't you like pie dough?"

"When it's baked, I do. Lots."

"Then Mr. Chipmunk will, too."

"Everything I like?"

"Everything."

"Would they like ice cream?"

"Of course."

"And cake?"

"Absolutely."

"And spinach?"

"If you like it, they like it."

"I don't like spinach."

"Well then, Mr. Chipmunk won't like it either."

"I'll get him to eat out of my hands," the boy said, and ran for the door. Before he opened it he slowed and peeked through the screen, but the chipmunk was not there, and he turned back to his grandmother. "He's gone."

"He'll come. You just wait and he'll come."

And so the boy went out quietly and sat on the steps with his hand to the side and the piece of pie-crust dough between his thumb and finger, and for a long time he did not see the chipmunk.

He heard birds singing and the constant roar of engines as the trucks moved somewhere out of sight and his grandmother singing some Norwegian song he could not understand, but he did not see the chipmunk for what seemed like hours. And then it came. Just as the boy began to give up and was about to go in and tell his grandmother it would not come, the chipmunk came.

FIVE

THE little red nose peeked out from beneath a log near the steps up to the cook trailer and when the boy didn't move the head came, and then the whole body.

For a second the chipmunk sat up on its hind legs, sat looking at him, making "chiccck" sounds in its throat, jerking its head at the boy, and when the boy still didn't move it came to the steps.

Up a little and back a little and up a little it would come, back and forth until it was on the same step as the boy, down at the other end.

It sat there for a full minute.

"Chicck, chicck." The chipmunk jerked and studied him, and he sat as still as he could, trying to not even breathe, and at last it was at the pie dough in his fingers.

There it stopped. Not two whiskers from the boy's fingers the chipmunk stopped and sat up again, looking directly into the boy's eyes, watching him, waiting for him to move.

And when the boy didn't, when he held as still as a piece of wood, the chipmunk leaned carefully forward, rested on one tiny paw, and used its mouth to pluck the piece of pie-crust dough out of the boy's fingers.

Then it ran with the dough, so fast the boy's eyes could not follow it—ran and disappeared back beneath the log.

"Phhhuuuuuu!" The boy's breath whistled out. It had eaten from his hand! He had never even seen one before and now a chipmunk had eaten out of his hand, and he ran in to tell his grandmother, and she laughed.

"I told you, my little thimble—if you like it, Mr. Chipmunk likes it."

He wished he had some spinach to see if Mr. Chipmunk would eat that, but he didn't say anything about spinach because he didn't want to know if there was any spinach. Instead he went to where she was rolling out pie crusts, with flour on her cheeks and in her hair, and he said:

"I do not know what a thimble is." He sat on the bench at the nearest eating table and looked up at her. "You call me your little thimble, but I don't know what a thimble is."

She looked at him for a moment, then smiled and went to a small wooden cheese box on a shelf above the stove. The corners of the box were fitted together like little fingers, and the name of the cheese was on the side of the box in red letters: VELVEETA.

She took the box down, and he could see that it was full of needles and spools of thread arranged in neat rows and by colors.

"See," she said. "See all of it and then see if you can pick out which one is a thimble."

He sat for a long time and picked through the objects in the box while she made pie crust and sang songs in Norwegian that he could not understand, and he finally found the thimble.

It was not that he knew what the thimble looked like but that it was the only thing left. He knew needles and thread, and he had seen his mother use a wooden embroidery hoop like the one stuck edgewise in the box, and at last there was nothing left in the box but the little silver cup-shaped object in the bottom. He picked it up and saw that the top of it was speckled in little dots, which he thought were supposed to be hair, because on the front of the object was the silver face of a fat little smiling boy. He held it closely so he could see it, and there was such detail that the eyes on the little silver boy had tiny, tiny lashes and there were little ears at the sides with earlobes.

"Is this the thimble?" he asked, holding it up, and she nodded.

"It is. And that's why I call you my little thimble—because you make me think of it."

"Do I look like the thimble?"

"You have the same dimples when you smile," she said.

"But not the speckled hair or the little silver ears and eyelashes."

"No, not that."

"What's it for?" he asked, and slipped it on the end of his finger when he said it, using it correctly without knowing it.

"Just that," she said. "To protect your finger

when you sew." She smiled and folded pie-crust dough over and over into itself. "To keep the needle from sticking you in the finger."

"Can I learn to sew?" The boy had seen his mother sew and now his grandmother talked of it, and he did not know what it meant to sew except that his mother pushed the needle back and forth through the cloth. "And wear the thimble?"

"I will teach you. All men must know how to sew in case they must live alone. I will teach you myself."

"When?"

"Tonight I will begin to teach you to sew, but now I must cook. You go outside the trailer and play for a time. But do not go in the woods or get near the machinery. I have to get ready for lunch."

"Can I take the thimble?"

"Yes. But don't lose it. I brought that all the way from the old country. My mother gave it to me and her mother gave it to her. You can play with it, but be careful."

He went outside and found a small patch of dirt next to the trailer, and he scooped some up and made a town for the thimble man. He used sticks and made bridges and roads and pretended that he was using the machinery, so he made machinery noises to mimic the sounds of the trucks he heard but did not see, because they were on the other side of some trees.

When he had roads and bridges he made a tiny house for the thimble man, and then he changed the game and thought of him as the thimble boy, because his grandmother had said he looked like the face on the thimble. He wondered how it would be to live in the small house of sticks and dirt.

"He has a little dog and a little cat and a little pet chipmunk so small we can't even see it," he said to himself. "And a little mother and father, and his father isn't away fighting in a war, and his mother doesn't make the sounds with Uncle Casey, and he's happy. He's always happy and he doesn't ride trains forever and ever. . . ."

The boy was crying and did not know it until some tears dripped on the side of the thimble boy's house and made the dirt crumble, and then he thought how could that be? How could he be crying when he didn't feel bad?

But he was, except that when he saw he was

crying the crying stopped and he went back to playing. He found when he lowered his face down to the dirt on its side and looked out of the eye closest to the ground the thimble boy and the thimble house and thimble play-ground became large, so huge he thought he could go into it and play.

"I could play with the thimble boy," he said, half-whispering. "We could play hide-and-seek and I could be It."

He hid the thimble boy so that he could not see him with the eye closest to the ground unless he moved sideways and looked down between a row of sticks he'd put in the dirt. "He's hiding in back of the wall. . . ."

"Who is?"

His grandmother had come to the door of the cook trailer to dump a pan of water, which she threw with great skill to the side to miss where the boy was playing.

"The thimble boy," he said, and explained how he was playing hide-and-seek.

"Do you have friends back in Chicago to play with?" she asked.

He shook his head. "No. No friends. Some-times Mother had Clara come and watch me while she went to work, but Clara didn't play with me. She was old and drank red wine from a big glass jar and listened to the radio. But she didn't play with me."

He started to tell her of Casey because once or twice Casey had tried to be nice to him and had tried to play with him and brought him toys—but he didn't. Instead, he squinted up at her—the sun was over her shoulder and he had trouble seeing her—and said, "I had a new truck and a tractor and a jeep to play with. They were all made of iron and had wheels that turned. I forgot them in Chicago. But I didn't have any friends to play with. Mother wouldn't let me play outside, because she said there are bad men who would hurt me."

He quit talking then. She was smiling down on him and it was the same smile she had when she first saw him at the depot, the kind of smile that made him feel soft inside and want to run to her and be hugged and held.

"Why don't you come into the trailer? I made some apple pies, and you can have a piece with some milk if you don't tell the men I gave you the first piece."

"Why can't I tell the men?"

Her eyes wrinkled at the corners and seemed to have a light in them, and she laughed a low laugh in her throat. "Because they always try to get the first piece for themselves. They say I'm going to marry whoever gets the first piece."

"Well, I'll marry you," he said, following her into the cook trailer. "So that takes care of that."

"Yes, that takes care of that." She picked him up and hugged him. "Now have some pie."

She took a pie down from the shelf over the sink where there were six pies cooling and put it on the table. He sat next to it and looked at it. It was a rich brown with some red mixed in with it and a little sugar sprinkled on it, and it smelled of apples and cinnamon, which he liked but could not say.

"It's got simmanon," he said. "It smells good."

She cut it with a knife cooled in water, and put a piece on a plate with a fork next to it, and sat down across from him.

"Aren't you going to eat pie?" he asked. She had no pie in front of her.

She shook her head. "Cooks never eat what they cook."

But she was smiling again and he knew she

was kidding him. He saw her eat during the day and it was what she had cooked. "You're so thin. Your arms are so thin. You should eat. That's what Mother tells me. She says I should eat or my arms will stay thin and I will never grow big like Uncle Casey."

He did not mean to speak of Uncle Casey, did not like to think of Uncle Casey even a little bit, but before he could stop, the name was out. He took a bite of the pie and chewed, looking down, but if his grandmother had heard the name she didn't say anything about it.

Instead she turned and went to the sink and poured some condensed milk from a can into a glass and added water and stirred it with a big spoon and brought it to him to drink with the pie. He thanked her and took a drink, and it tasted like tin from the can, tin and something else he couldn't name, but it was still good, and when the taste mixed with the taste of the apple pie in his mouth even the tin in the milk went away.

The boy ate quietly for a time, tasting each bite and drinking the warm milk and thinking of all the things that were in the pie—the sugar and cinnamon and dough and juice and apples—and he could not understand how it could all come together and make a pie that would taste so good.

"There's so many things in it," he said to his grandmother around a bite on the fork.

"In what?"

"In the pie. So many different things and they aren't all good, but when they are in the pie they are good.

"What isn't good?"

"Apples aren't good, because they hurt your teeth when you bite them. And simmanon is too strong. And sugar makes you sick if you eat too much of it. I ate some once from a spoon from a sack when Mother was at work and Clara wasn't watching and I threw up."

"I don't understand you."

"When you put them all together in a pie they taste good and make me want to eat more and more and even drink the milk with the tin in it. How can that be?"

His grandmother leaned back in the bench across the table and smiled. "You think so strange about things. . . ."

But she didn't answer the question about

the pie. Instead she stood and cut him another small piece and he ate that as well until his stomach felt tight and round with it.

"Maybe it is time for a little rest," she said then, putting the plate near the bucket of water and the washbasin. She sat on the bunk and wiggled her finger for him to come over, and he went to her and sat on the bed.

She used her hand to wipe his forehead once and then once again and the motion made him drowsy so that he let her put him back on the pillow and lie next to him and sing.

She sang a soft song in Norwegian that he couldn't understand. The small sounds seemed to be inside his head and in the pillow and in his hair.

And he could not stay awake.

He wanted an answer to the question about the pie and the things that made a pie, because it seemed important to know how to take many things that aren't so good and make one good thing with them.

But the small sounds of the song took him and he could not think any longer.

SIX

THE BOY dreamed of going to a zoo with his mother. There were lions and snakes and tigers and elephants all in dusty cages, and his mother held his hand to lead him through. They looked at each one and his mother smiled and held his hand.

When they came to the monkey cage one of the monkeys made a face at him, and he made a face back and looked up at his mother to show her the face.

Except that it wasn't his mother anymore but had turned into Uncle Casey and he was holding the boy's hand and smiling.

Smiling down on the boy.

And it wasn't a bad smile. It was a happy smile, and the boy smiled back, but Uncle Casey was holding his hand hard, really hard, so hard the boy almost cried out, so hard and harder and harder until the boy could not stand it.

His eyes snapped open and for a second time he did not know where he was—felt himself still in the zoo being held too hard by Uncle Casey.

Then he heard his grandmother singing and saw the end of the wood stove and knew he was all right.

He sat up and rubbed his eyes.

"Are we awake?" His grandmother peered around the end of the stove.

"I had a dream," he said. "I was at the zoo with Mother and we saw tigers and snakes and monkeys and Mother was holding my hand and she turned into . . ."

He stopped. He didn't want to talk about Uncle Casey and once again his grandmother acted as if nothing were wrong.

"The men will be in soon and they will be hungry. After they eat maybe you can ask them the question about how bad things can make good things. Now help me set the tables before they get here."

The boy took the plates and silverware and laid them out on the tables, but he did not think he would dare to ask the men any questions. Then he put all the cups upside down and arranged them in neat lines so they lined up with each other and all the other cups and plates on the other tables.

And then the men came.

It was as before.

The boy wasn't ready and in some way they frightened him. They were so huge as they came in that he couldn't help moving in back of his grandmother's dress until they were all seated.

Then they had to eat, and he helped take food to them. Bowl after bowl of potatoes and gravy and strips of meat in the gravy and they ate and ate until the boy could do nothing but stand around in back of the stove and watch them until there was no food left.

When they were done eating meat and potatocs they drank coffee, and the boy helped bring them pie and each of them ate a giant piece of pie and drank another cup of coffee. His grandmother handed him a box of sugar lumps for each table. She poured them still more coffee, hot and steaming, and the men sat for a time holding sugar lumps in their coffee.

It looked so strange to him, their huge fingers holding the tiny sugar lumps in each cup like little toys. When a lump had soaked up coffee until it was brown and almost ready to crumble, each man would carefully put it on his tongue and take a sip of coffee noisily, wash the lump around, then swallow it.

And take another lump and do it again.

The boy watched them until all had finished their coffee and he thought they were done. He wanted them to be done because he had about a thousand questions to ask his grandmother.

Like, Why were they so big?

And, How could they eat so much?

And, Why were their faces two colors?

And, Why did they dip the sugar cubes in coffee and suck them to nothing in their mouths and always take their caps off and jam them in their pockets when they came in and always spit in the can by the door and clean out their lower lips with their fingers, and talk so loud it made his ears hurt, but they didn't leave.

They didn't leave at all as they had in the morning.

Instead when they finished eating they pushed their plates away for the boy and his grandmother to clear off.

They laughed and told jokes about the day while the boy took the plates away and they made an effort to ruffle his blond hair when he went by, and asked to see his muscles.

SEVEN

WHEN the tables were cleared they leaned back in their chairs and filled their lower lips with tobacco from the little round cans in their bib overalls.

Then they took out small decks of cards— or at least they looked small in their large hands. They broke into two groups and they began to deal and play cards.

The boy and his grandmother sat by the stove and watched them. She had saved a plate for him, and he ate potatoes and meat without looking, taking food and chewing it and swallowing without thinking as he watched the men.

He did not know about cards, did not know how to play with them, except once alone in the apartment when Clara was drunk and his mother was gone to work Clara had shown him how to build a house with cards.

He had tried hard, but the card house kept falling. At first Clara had laughed at him, but then she grew angry and threw all the cards in the garbage, and that was all he knew about cards.

The men weren't building houses anyway.

They would deal all the cards around; then they would throw them down one at a time.

One man would start by throwing a card down, then each of the other men in the group threw a card down with a great slap of the card and a loud laugh or curse.

"There! I've got you, by God!" they would yell, and slap a card down so hard the tables jumped off the floor.

"What is this game?" the boy asked his grandmother when he dared. He spoke in a whisper, afraid to disturb the men.

"It's called whist," she said.

"Why does it make them mad?" he whispered directly into her ear so they would not hear.

"Mad? They aren't mad."

"But they're so loud and throw the cards down so hard . . ."

But she did not hear him. She had signaled one of the men with her fingers. "Gustaf— the boy knows nothing of whist. Show him, will you?"

And Gustaf, who had a face of two colors and a scar on one cheek that made his eye droop and was almost bald, smiled at the boy.

"Come and sit on my lap, boy, and help me whip these buggers."

But the boy was shy and would not have done it—was shy and afraid—except that his grandmother grabbed him by the hand and half guided, half dragged him to the man named Gustaf.

Gustaf scooped the boy up in his huge arm and propped him on his lap with his arms around him, holding him in.

"Deal, boys," Gustaf said, his voice so deep that his chest rumbled against the boy's back.

The boy smelled the pungent odor of snoose and trees and oily diesel smoke in Gustaf. And somehow he could not separate the smells from the sounds he had heard of the trucks; the roar of the engines was in the big man's smell, and the boy thought how safe it was to be in his lap. Like being in his grandmother's lap or his mother's lap.

Gustaf picked up his cards as they were dealt. The boy looked at the pictures on the cards and the little symbols and numbers, and it was before he knew numbers, but he thought they were pretty anyway and he smiled up at Gustaf.

"Good, aren't they?" Gustaf said, and winked.

Then he played, and each time he leaned forward to slap a card down on top of another man's card it rocked the boy forward gently— forward like a cradle would rock him, safe in Gustaf's arms.

Soon all the men's talk flowed together and made one long sound, and the rocking forward became one with the sound and the safe place, and he was so comfortable that the cards seemed to blur.

He could not keep his eyes open, and he fell asleep caught between Gustaf's big arms. He missed all the rest of the game, slept with his head over on Gustaf's arm, and when it was over Gustaf lifted him to carry him to bed in back of the stove.

"He's light as a goose down pillow," Gustaf said, putting him in the bunk. "Tomorrow I'll take him on the cat with me—he needs to work. Get some weight to him."

That the boy heard through the sleep. And though the words didn't cause him to awaken, they did make his sleep move into dreams of wonder at what it would be like to go to work with Gustaf. . . .

EIGHT

THE BOY awakened early because he was excited. It was still dark outside—he could not see anything through the windows. But early as it was his grandmother was already awake. She had a small mirror hung on a nail by the sink, and she was looking in the mirror while she braided her hair, which hung down in long ropes, the gray like frosting mixed with black cake, hung down to her waist, and she braided it while he watched, with graceful movements of her hands.

One over the other over the other over the other, he thought; her hands move like small birds flying one over the other over the other over the other.

He loved to watch her comb and braid her hair. She was his grandmother and very old, but when she combed and braided her hair he thought she looked like a girl next door in the Chicago apartment who combed her hair and braided it on the back stoop.

His grandmother saw him watching and smiled at him.

"Why are you up so early, little thimble?" she asked.

"Gustaf said he would take me on the cat."

"Oh—you heard. I thought you were asleep when he said that." The braid was done and she raised it over her head and coiled it in back at the top of her head.

The boy sat up, stood by the stove. "Did he mean it? Is he really going to take me with him?"

She winked. "I don't know—what do you think?"

"Oh, Grandma, you're teasing me."

"I am, am I?"

"Aren't you?"

"Come now." She used a ladle to put steaming oatmeal in a bowl. "Eat some breakfast." She mixed milk in a bowl and poured it on the oatmeal. "So you will be done eating when the men come."

The boy sat in front of the bowl and ate with a large spoon. The oatmeal was very hot and it made the milk smell funny, but he sprinkled sugar on it and held his breath and ate and it tasted good.

He had just finished eating when the door burst open and the men came in for breakfast, and he was kept busy running back and forth with bowls of oatmeal and pancakes.

But he kept his eye always on Gustaf who ate and ate. When the men were done they all stood up and thanked his grandmother and moved out of the cook trailer.

Gustaf went with them and the boy felt the edges of disappointment.

Except that at the door Gustaf stopped and turned.

"Well?" He smiled and winked at the boy's grandmother, then looked at the boy. "Aren't you coming?"

The boy looked up at his grandmother. She nodded and he ran to the door.

Gustaf took him around the waist, lifted him, and went out the door carrying the boy on his arm.

OUTSIDE the other men had gone down a path through some trees, and in a moment the roar of diesel engines filled the air.

Gustaf moved off in another direction, the boy on his arm. They walked down a narrow road through the trees until they came to a large clearing.

In the middle of the clearing was an enormous gravel pile. The boy had never seen anything so huge.

"I can't see over it," he said to Gustaf. "What is it?"

"It's the gravel pile," Gustaf said. "For building the road. The cat is around the other side. . . ."

The boy was so excited he could hardly bear it. As they walked around the side of the pile that went to the sky, the boy saw a big caterpillar tractor parked at the bottom of the pile.

Gustaf walked to the side of the cat and put the boy up on top of the steel treads next to the driver's seat.

Everything was yellow and oily and there were levers and dials all over the tractor. He stood on the treads and did not dare touch anything.

"Hang on to the seat," Gustaf said, "while I climb up."

The boy did as he was told.

Gustaf went around the cat. He stopped and did something to the engine, then climbed into the seat and put the boy on his lap between his arms.

The boy leaned back.

Gustaf's hands flew across the controls, hitting levers and switches, and there was a sudden roar as the engine caught and started. Blue flame splatted up out of the exhaust pipe, and the boy jumped.

The engine roar grew louder and louder still, and Gustaf's hands moved again and the bulldozer, the cat, suddenly lurched forward.

The boy closed his eyes, then opened them once more. They were climbing up the face of the gravel pile. Gustaf's strong hands worked the two steering levers and guided the bulldozer up and up the gravel pile until it came to the top.

The boy almost fainted. They were high, so

high he could see all around. He saw the cook trailer where his grandmother was working and the trees that went on and on forever, and out in front of the pile, below and to the right, were all the dump trucks in a line.

At the bottom of the gravel pile was a large grate made of heavy steel. Trucks would pull beneath the grate and gravel would pour down until the truck was filled.

There was a truck beneath the grate now, waiting, and before the boy was ready, before the boy could think what was happening, Gustaf made the engine roar louder, worked a lever so the huge blade lowered, and the cat roared over the top of the pile and down, down toward the grate, toward the hole.

The move was so sudden that it made the boy scream and grab at Gustaf's arm. But the sound of the engine covered his scream.

It seemed they couldn't keep from tipping over to the front, so steep was the side of the gravel pile.

The cat roared down on the grate and hole with the blade pushing a huge pile of gravel. When the gravel hit the grate it dropped through and disappeared in a great cloud of dust and *whump*ed down into a dump truck.

The truck moved away and another truck took its place. But before the boy could really see what was happening, Gustaf's hands worked the levers and the cat stopped dead and suddenly slammed backward up the pile again.

To the top.

To teeter on the top and hold for a moment, seeming to fall and then . . .

Down again to pour another load off the blade into the hole, and another truck filled and jerked away.

And back to the top.

"It's like a ride," the boy yelled up at Gustaf. "At the fair." He had once been to a fair, and his mother had taken him for a ride on a small roller coaster where she held him. "It's like the roller coaster."

This time he yelled his loudest and Gustaf heard him. He smiled and spit over the treads. "Yah, yah. It's fun, ha?"

But there was no time to answer, because Gustaf had worked the levers and the cat was barreling down again.

Except that this time Gustaf grabbed the boy's hands and put them on the levers beneath his own, held them inside his hands and then let the boy steer the cat as it backed up the pile, and again held the boy's hands on other levers to shift and throttle the cat down with another load.

All morning.

He sat in Gustaf's lap all morning loading the trucks with gravel to make the road.

When it was midday the boy was covered with dust and dirt and half-deaf from the roar of the engine and had never been so happy in his life.

"We must eat now," Gustaf said, turning the cat engine off. "Then there is more work, yah?"

NINE

THE BOY followed Gustaf as he walked to the cook trailer. All the other men had stopped the trucks and were walking to the cook trailer as well, and the boy walked with them trying to walk as they walked, with his shoulders back and taking long steps, and he spit and cleared his lip like the men.

He had so much to tell his grandmother about the gravel pile and the cat and how it tipped up and down and frightened him, and when he came into the cook trailer he ran to her.

She was at the stove and smiled at him. "You're dirty."

"Oh, Grandma, I rode the cat and Gustaf put my hands on the levers and I got to drive and steer and raise and lower the blade and we rode to the top of the gravel pile and down . . ."

All the words ran together and his grandmother held up her hand.

"Later. Tell me all of it later. Now you have to eat."

The men trooped in and took their caps off, slammed them against their legs to knock the dust off, and the boy did the same with his hands, wishing he had a greasy cap to slam against his leg. He moved to the stove to eat sitting on the bunk—except that he didn't eat at the stove as he had before, didn't have to wait until the men were done, didn't have to help with the tables this time.

"When we are men we must eat with the men," Gustaf said, and motioned to an extra plate next to his on the table. Other men nodded and smiled, and the boy went to the bench and sat at the plate and looked at his grandmother, who also smiled and nodded.

He tried to make himself bigger, but he

could not, and still he felt proud that he could sit with the men, although he noticed that one of them, a man named Olaf, helped his grandmother bring food to the tables.

Gustaf heaped food on the boy's plate and he tried to eat it all but could not, could not eat even a part of as much as the men ate, and when he was so full with stew his stomach was about to burst he looked up at Gustaf.

"I can't eat more."

"Then you shouldn't have taken it," Gustaf said, but he was smiling, and he used his fork to scrape the boy's food onto his own plate, from which it quickly disappeared.

The boy was so full he could not eat pie. When they were done Gustaf started to leave, to go back to the cat and the boy started to follow, but Carl, the man who had come to the depot to get him, stopped him with his hand.

"Gustaf doesn't get you all the time. I need help driving the dump truck this afternoon."

The boy looked at Gustaf who nodded. "We must share you—good men are hard to find." And the boy knew he was joking, but it still sounded nice.

Again he looked to his grandmother to see

that it was all right, and again she smiled and nodded, and he went out with Carl.

It was the same truck they had come in from the depot, but he was not asleep this time and there was much, much more happening for him to see.

Carl's truck was third in line. The boy watched the other trucks drive under the grate and watched Gustaf on the cat push the loads of gravel down the pile into the trucks where they landed with great noises and clouds of dust.

Finally it was Carl's turn, and he growl-whined the truck forward under the grate. The boy tried to lean over Carl and see Gustaf use the cat, but it was too far back and up to see through the grate.

Suddenly the truck lurched sideways as the load of gravel dropped down into it, and no sooner had the dust begun to settle on them, bouncing off the hood, than Carl worked the levers and the throttle and the truck whined forward.

And out of the gravel pile place and down a long dirt road with new gravel on it, fresh and damp looking to the boy, like cereal; out and down the road where they met other trucks coming back empty until they reached the end of the road. . . .

Where there were two more cats and a grader. The bulldozers would plow the trees over with their big blades, and when the trees were gone the gravel trucks ahead of Carl's truck would dump their loads and the grader would even it out.

Finally it was Carl's turn. The last truck dumped with a great raising and sliding sound and turned and headed back to the gravel pile, and Carl moved his truck forward. When it was in the right position he reached out the window and pulled a lever with a rope on it and the bed of the truck *whoosh*ed and raised slowly.

The boy could feel the gravel slide out of the truck onto the ground, feel the truck bounce as the weight left it and Carl pulled the lever and turned the truck around while the empty box was coming back down, and then he started the long journey back to the gravel pile—except that he turned to the boy and said:

"Do you want to drive?"

He made room in his lap for the boy, who moved to sit there and hold the wheel and steer it under Carl's hands as he had steered the cat under Gustaf's hands, and they met trucks and saw a deer, and he steered and didn't have to make engine sounds with his mouth because the truck made them fine without him.

All the way back he steered and into line for the next load, and he thought of all the things he had seen and done, all the many things he had seen and done this day that he could tell his grandmother about tonight when they had apple pie and the milk with the taste of tin in it.

TEN

THEY had eaten supper and all the men had gone to the sleeping trailer, and the boy sat with his grandmother at a table.

It was dark and he was very tircd, but she had given him a piece of cherry pie she'd made with canned filling and a glass of the warm milk that tasted of tin, and he was trying to remember all the things of the day to tell her.

"It was so much fun," he said. "I drove the cat first and then the truck and steered and worked the shift lever. Carl let me sit in his lap and spit out the window and wear his cap with the button on it and press the horn, except that it didn't work."

"Eat your pie," she said, pushing his hair away from his forehead with the back with her hand. It was a soft touch, like a kiss with her fingers, and he paused and ate a piece of pie but could not stop telling her of the day, and before he knew it, before he could stop himself, he had said things about Uncle Casey.

"We had fun, too," he said. "Uncle Casey took me to the zoo once and to a movie where cowboys rode and jumped on a stagecoach and shot the guns out of other cowboys' hands and I thought I would never have as much fun as I did with Uncle Casey. But then he and Mother made the sounds on the couch and I didn't have fun with Uncle Casey anymore, but it doesn't matter now. Now I'm having more fun with Gustaf and Carl and you than I ever had with Uncle Casey. . . ."

His grandmother's face had changed. The smile was still there but it had become tight, and the edges of her eyes looked hard so that the boy trailed off and could not say more. It was anger, but more, too—she was more than mad. He thought something must hurt her, and he knew it was what he had said but did not know why it would have hurt her to say he had fun with Uncle Casey.

She stood from the table and turned away from him and picked up the flyswatter that hung by the stove. It was the kind of swatter that was made from a screen and had a picture of a circus clown on it and a red wire handle, and she went to the window over the sink and hit a fly.

Small hits, the boy saw. She used little flicks of her wrist, and even when he did not see the fly a fly would fall.

She didn't say anything for a long time, just went around the trailer flicking at the flies, dropping them on the floor, and when she was done—the boy watched her the whole time— she took the broom and dustpan and swept each fly body up to dump in the wood stove.

She is thinking of something else, the boy thought, watching her kill flies; as when his mother would speak to him but be looking at something else, not thinking about what she was saying.

His grandmother was killing the flies but not seeing them, not thinking of them, not caring about them except to kill them, and when she was done she turned to the boy once more and sat at the table and pushed the hair away from his forehead.

"Tell me," she said, "about Uncle Casey. Do you like him?"

So the boy finished his cherry pie and warm milk and tried to think first if he liked Uncle Casey or not and decided he did not.

"But he is fun," the boy said. "Sometimes he takes me to movies and we go to the Cozy Corner and he drinks beer with Mother and gives me nickels for the jukebox and fried chicken. . . . And he took me to the zoo and we laughed at the monkeys."

"But you don't like him?"

"No. I don't like him. Sometimes he looks at Mother and doesn't see me, and when they are together . . . well, I just don't like him."

And again her face grew tight, but this time she did not get up or move away. "It's late now. Why don't you go to bed?"

"Aren't you coming to bed?"

"No. I have some things to do to get ready for tomorrow."

She helped him to bed and tucked him in and kissed him on the forehead, and he could smell the lavender water she used in the morning on her neck, and he fell almost asleep.

She sang softly for him with her hand on his forehead and his eyes closed. It was a song about a young girl, and she did not sing it in Norwegian but in English so he could understand. The song was sad and in a story and he wanted to hear it, but sleep came before she reached the end of the song and he did not hear more.

HE DID NOT know how long he slept, but he awakened before morning. A strange sound cut through his sleep, and he opened his eyes.

His grandmother was sitting at the table nearest the stove. She had an oil lamp on the table and a small tablet and a stub of a pencil in her hand. She was wearing small glasses that sat on the end of her nose, and she was writing on the tablet, the pencil making tiny scratching sounds.

And while she wrote she talked, spoke down to the paper.

"Damn war," she said. "Damn the war and damn the men and damn the cities that take the girls."

And here her voice changed and became lilting and high and made the boy think of his mother.

"Remember who you are," his grandmother said, the little pencil squiggling. "And how it was before the war when the men were different. You mustn't be this way. . . ."

And she was crying down onto the tablet, tears dropping on the paper.

The boy started to say something, tell her he was awake, but he held back. Something about her tears stopped him from making a sound, and instead he got out of bed quietly and went to her and hugged her.

"It's all right, Grandma. . . ."

She held him. "I know. Everything will be all right. You'll see."

Which made no sense to him, because he had just had a day when he drove the cat and steered the truck and everything was already as all right as it could be, but he said nothing.

She put him back to bed and combed her hair down and came to bed herself, and he fell asleep almost at once and did not awaken until the men came in for breakfast.

ELEVEN

FOR DAYS things got better and better and better. . . .

Carl let him drive the truck again and spit out the window, and then all the other men seemed to want him, and he rode in their trucks as well until he knew them all.

Sven, Ole, Nels, Harvey, Emil, Altag, Pete—he knew all their names and the way they laughed and joked and spit and wore their caps.

He rode with them all and drove the gravel pile cat again and drove everything but the cat that cleared the forest ahead of the grader so there could be a road; he rode with everybody except the road cat, and each night when they were done eating and the men had gone to the sleeping trailer he would sit and eat pie and drink milk and tell his grandmother all about each day before he went to bed.

And each night she would stay up when he was in bed and write a letter, which she put in her apron pocket.

There was one for each day, one letter in a small envelope for each day and each night she cried and swore and killed flies even when there were no flies and came to bed when she was done.

ON FRIDAY Carl came to her instead of going to work with his truck. The boy was sitting at a table finishing his oatmeal, and he looked up at Carl, thinking the truck driver wanted to take him with him to work again.

But this day was different.

"It is time to go to town," Carl said. "I'll warm the truck and you and the boy get ready."

Once a week they had to go to a town that

lay thirty miles away by rutted narrow road, and the boy had not known it.

They had to go to buy supplies for the camp.

"Where are we going?" he asked as they walked to Carl's truck. "Why aren't we going to work?"

"We're going to Salvang," his grandmother said. "We need food."

"For the men?"

"And you."

"Is there a store in Salvang?"

"Yes."

They climbed into the truck and Carl started driving down the dirt road, shifting through the whining gears.

It was a beautiful morning with a clear blue sky. The trees along the road were so green in the morning sun they hurt the boy's eyes.

For a short time Carl drove down the same road the boy had come on from the depot and he thought he remembered the way.

But then they turned off onto a side road that was worse than the one they'd been on, and soon it was so rough the truck bounced from side to side.

They came to a stream, and the road disappeared into the water, and Carl drove the truck right through the stream.

They saw a moose. It was huge and brown, standing in the middle of the road, and it did not move until Carl beeped the truck's horn—and then it only walked slowly away, all but ignoring the truck and the horn.

When it seemed to the boy that they would never get out of the woods, the trees suddenly fell away from the road and opened into cleared fields and farms.

In the distance he saw a metal water tower with a word written on the side. He couldn't read the word, but his grandmother leaned over and said, "It's Salvang," into his ear so he could hear it.

It was a small town. After Chicago and the apartment buildings, Salvang was almost not a town at all.

"One, two, three, four, five," the boy said. "Five houses I count."

And that was all of Salvang. Five houses and one store where Carl stopped the truck. But when the boy followed his grandmother and Carl inside he saw it was like no other store he'd ever seen.

The store seemed to sell everything in the whole world.

Inside it was dark and cool and there was a high ceiling made of molded metal all pressed in a design with flowers in it. The boy stared at the ceiling while his grandmother talked to the man who owned the store—stared until he became dizzy and had to hold his grand-mother's dress to keep from falling over.

He looked down at the walls, but there were so many things to see he still had to close his eyes to stop the dizziness.

There were buckets and tubs and axes and ladders and leather harnesses and bags of feed stacked higher than even Carl could have reached. There were rolls of brightly colored cloth and layers of canvas belting and stacks of cans of food and a huge metal bin with a picture of crackers on the side.

And a glass counter full of pocket watches and pocketknives.

"Oh," the boy said, because on top of the counter was a large glass jar of candy. "Oh," he said again, and pulled on his grandmother's dress. "See it?"

She nodded and put her hand on his head,

yet seemed not to hear. But the store owner looked down at him and smiled and handed the jar down.

The boy looked up at his grandmother and she said:

"Go ahead."

He took a green candy with red stripes and held it up to the light to see the colors before he put it in his mouth.

It was very sweet with a sharpness in the green part that made his tongue feel cool.

He sucked on the candy slowly, hanging on to his grandmother's dress, and she told the store owner all the things she needed:

"Potatoes, one hundred and fifty pounds, and the same of flour and some yeast and five gallons of syrup and thirty cans of tomatoes. . . ."

Her voice went on as she read from the list, but the boy didn't really listen until the very end.

At the end of the list she said:

"I want the smallest engineer cap you have and also the smallest set of children's bib overalls you can find. For the boy."

"And that pocketknife in the case," Carl said. He was leaning over the glass counter.

"The one with the black handle and the eagle on it."

The storekeeper took the knife out of the case and handed it to Carl.

Carl turned to the boy. "Here—don't cut yourself."

The boy couldn't believe that Carl had given him the knife. He held it tightly in his hand and looked at it closely.

It had two bright silver blades and a shiny black handle. On the handle was a picture of an eagle holding arrows in its talons.

It was the most beautiful thing the boy had ever seen.

"Thank you," he said to Carl. "It's so pretty." He turned to his grandmother. "See how the eagle shines?"

She nodded and smiled and pushed the hair out of his eyes but was still speaking to the store owner again.

"I need to mail some letters," she said to him. "Can you do that?"

The store owner nodded. "They go out every Monday."

"She's down in Chicago," the boy's grandmother explained. "Will the letters go that far?"

"Absolutely."

"Good. Here." She handed him all the letters she had written through the week sitting at the table each night.

From her apron pocket she took a coin purse and gave the store owner change for stamps.

"Mail them," she said, her voice tight. "Mail them good and hard."

"I will," the store owner said.

Then the owner and Carl loaded all the groceries in the back of the dump truck by lifting the tailgate.

Then his grandmother, Carl, and the boy traveled back to camp the same way they had come, but the boy saw none of the country.

He sat the whole way back holding the knife in his hand, turning it this way and that so the light shone on the eagle.

It was so beautiful—the most beautiful of all things—and he suddenly wished that he was with his mother so he could show her the knife. He missed her so much it hurt but he said nothing, just sat between Carl and his grandmother looking at the knife.

TWELVE

THE BOY thought life in the cook-camp could just go on and on except for missing his mother.

Summer days mixed with summer nights in the cook trailer and it all seemed to be more of a home than even Chicago was a home except for missing his mother.

In the days he would either ride with the men in the trucks or on the cat or play outside the trailer and use the pocketknife with the eagle on it to make little wooden houses or stick fences and stick animals and he only cut himself two or three times, when he would go crying in to his grandmother to get a bandage, and that was all right except for missing his mother.

In the evenings he would sit with his grandmother after the men had gone to the sleeping trailer and eat pie and drink warm milk made from the can and swat at the mice that ran around on the floor with a broom and listen to her sing songs about her childhood in Norway, and that was all right except for missing his mother.

And the days could have gone on and on, the boy thought, except that as the men made it, the road went farther and farther from the camp, and they had to move the cook trailer and sleeping trailer to get closer to the end of the road so they didn't have to drive so far to sleep or eat.

Moving day was a time of large excitement. He helped his grandmother pack dish towels around all the dishes in the cupboards and tape all the drawers and doors shut and lift the steps to the cook trailer and put them in on the floor.

Then the men hooked the trailer to one of the trucks with a steel pin and they drove down the road with the boy and his grand-mother sitting in the truck. The boy tried to see the trailer out the back window of the truck to watch it being pulled, but the dump box blocked the way and he couldn't see it. Carl noticed him and put him in his lap, from which the boy could watch in the outside mir-ror as the trailer bumped and bounced down the road in back of the truck.

He thought how strange it was to watch your whole house bouncing down the road, and he thought of the chairs inside and all the wrapped dishes and his bed bouncing and bouncing as they drove down the road.

"What about the mice?" he asked his grand-mother.

"What?" She had been speaking to Carl and had not heard him.

"What about all the mice in the cook trailer? When we get to the new place they won't know how they got there. Their whole house is bouncing away. What about them?"

Carl laughed and his grandmother smiled.

"They take their home with them," she said, "just like us. They have beds and nests in the trailer and it doesn't matter where they are—that's their home."

Just like me, the boy thought but didn't say it and missed his mother.

"I miss Mother," he said, but the words were lost in the grind and whine of the truck motor, and his grandmother didn't hear them.

It took almost an hour to get to the new place for the trailer and then another half hour to back it into position and get it level. All the men helped by grabbing the hitch and the corners and rocking it around until it was straight and they could set up the steps.

As soon as the trailer was in place the boy ran inside to see what had changed, but nothing had fallen or broken. Everything looked as they had left it before they started to move.

"We have to pull all the tape from the drawers and doors," his grandmother said, "and get food ready for supper."

He helped pull the tape and wad it into a sticky ball and set all the salt shakers out on the tables and get the chairs straight and was just starting with the pepper shakers when there was a loud yell from outside and two men came in the door carrying a third man between them.

"Clear a table!" one of the men yelled to

the boy. "A tree fell on Harvey and crushed his arm. He's out cold."

The boy stood frozen, looking at the man hanging between the other two, and he wondered if the man was dead. He looked white, as white as the milk from the cans, and his eyes were open and showed white as well. His grandmother stepped around the boy, moving very fast, pushed the salt shaker to the end of the table, and helped them put Harvey on his back along the tabletop.

"Get his legs up," his grandmother said. "Hold them up."

One of the men took Harvey's legs and held them with Harvey's ankles on his shoulders.

"A tree backed," the other man said, "came back down across the cat and through the cage. It caught his arm on the side rest."

And the boy saw that his arm was mangled and crushed and bleeding. His grandmother worked so fast that her hands were almost a blur. She found scissors and cut the sleeve away from his shirt and cut it away from the wound and brought some water in a pan with a dish towel and washed it as best she could. Then she found some tape in a drawer and her breadboard that she used for kneading dough to make the bread.

"Raise him," she said to the men and they lifted Harvey up enough so she could slide the board under his elbow and she taped the arm to the board and then the board to his body, taped and taped, and all of it the boy watched.

Then, because his legs were raised, Harvey came to and his eyes focused, but he couldn't say anything. He grunted with it and swore and did not see even that there were other people in the room but just kept grunting with the pain and swearing in a low voice.

"We have to get him back to the depot," the boy's grandmother said, "and down by train to Pinewood to the doctor."

"I'll take him," Carl said. He had come in.

The boy's grandmother nodded. "I'll have to go as well, in case he goes back into shock from the movement."

"What about the boy?" Carl said. "We could be gone two days, waiting for a train."

"He'll stay with the men," she said, and looked at the boy. "You'll be all right, won't you?"

And he nodded without thinking what he was doing, still watching the man on the table, seeing his eyes dull with pain and the blood on his arm and the table, and wondering how it could be that anything could hurt that much and the man not cry and ask for his mother.

"You'll be all right," his grandmother repeated. "You can sleep tonight and tomorrow night in the sleeping trailer with the men."

Harvey grunted again, this time ending with a small whine, and she motioned to the door. "Take him out now. I'll follow."

They carried him out, three men this time, one to hold the crushed arm, and the boy followed them, trying to see all the things there were to see, trying to see Harvey's face again because it looked so strange, but they were gone too fast.

They loaded him in the front of Carl's truck, and Carl and the boy's grandmother got in, one on each side to hold Harvey up between them, and they started the long drive to the depot, and the boy watched them leave, watched them drive away until the truck was nothing but a small dot between the rows of trees on the new gravel road.

Then he turned to the cook trailer. All the other men had gone to their trucks and back to work and he went into the cook trailer and sat alone at the table for a time and missed his mother.

But she was not there, and after a little more time had passed he took out his pocketknife and looked at the eagle and went outside to find a stick to carve smooth as he'd seen some of the men do, and in this way he kept busy all afternoon until the men finished working and came to eat supper. Gustaf came first.

"Is the food ready?" Gustaf asked him when he came up to the cook trailer and found the boy sitting outside.

"No. I don't know how to do it."

"Well, come and help me and learn then, boy," Gustaf said, and smiled. "Then you can make slum stew for us tomorrow."

Of course the boy knew Gustaf was just joking, that he wouldn't really have to cook, but he followed Gustaf in and set the tables while Gustaf fired up the stove.

He put a huge pot on the stove and peeled potatoes, and the boy helped him peel, watching his pocketknife take the gray skin off in short, thick pieces while Gustaf's peelings came off long and thin.

When the pot was nearly full of potatoes Gustaf added a can of some kind of meat and cans of carrots and put the lid on and made a large pot of coffee while they waited.

"Ever have coffee, boy?" Gustaf asked, and when the boy shook his head he poured coffee into a thick cup with two spoonfuls of sugar and canned milk and stirred it and handed it to the boy.

The boy sipped it, expecting to burn his tongue, but the milk had cooled the coffee and it tasted like thick, sweet almost-chocolate.

"It's good," he said to Gustaf. "Sweet . . ."

"Just one cup. It will stunt your growth and you'll never get big enough to drive the trucks yourself."

Of course the boy did not believe Gustaf because all the men drank coffee and none of them had stunted their growth or they wouldn't have seemed large as houses when they came in the trailer, but they did not talk more and sat drinking the coffee, the boy feeling the edges of being a man, until the other men came in to eat the stew Gustaf and the boy had made.

THIRTEEN

H<small>E TRIED</small> to eat with the men again, eat as much as they ate because he had to be with them alone, but he could not.

They ate stew with salt and pepper thick on it, ate it with spoons and joked about how bad Gustaf and the boy were as cooks, which was only partly true.

When they were done eating and the men had used their fingers to wipe out the pot, licking them clean, they all leaned back and put snoose in their lower lips and sat to talk for a little time.

The boy tried to listen, but it was all talk older than he could understand.

"She's using oil now worse than ever—I think her rings are gone."

"My dump is taking so long I could take a nap while she gets rid of her load."

It all swam in his head. Talk of valves and fluids and yards of gravel and Harvey's arm went into his ears, but the room was warm and his stomach was full and nothing made sense to him.

His eyes closed and he would have slept, leaning against Gustaf, except that Gustaf picked him up and carried him to the sleeping trailer.

"Big day for little ones," Gustaf said, and though it wasn't dark yet he tucked the boy into Harvey's bunk.

The bunk smelled of man sweat—almost a stink but still nice in the boy's nose—and he fell asleep wondering about Harvey's arm and missing his mother.

Always that—missing his mother. Even in sleep.

He did not sleep well. Gustaf put him to bed so early it was just barely dark. For a time he seemed to sleep hard, but in the darkness his eyes snapped open and he lay for a moment trying to remember where he was.

Around him there were all the sounds of the men breathing and snoring and rasping, and he was frightened because it sounded like monsters and he could see monsters in all the shadows in the trailer. Moving with the moonlight that came through the windows in slanted gray bars, they seemed to dance around the room on the walls; the monsters, not the men, seemed to be making the sounds and he sat up and closed his eyes.

When he opened them he could see the other bunks with the men sleeping and smell the men sleeping and hear that it was the men making sounds and the monsters were gone.

The trailer was so strange.

There was nothing soft in the men's sleeping trailer. In the cook trailer with his grandmother there were curtains on the windows and a fresh smell of lavender water and bread cooking and brown sugar and here it was all hard. The windows had no covers, no curtains, no soft edges, and the sounds and smells were thick somehow.

But it did not frighten him any longer, and

he went back to sleep with the blanket wrapped around him.

In the morning he was awakened by coughing and spitting. It seemed that every man woke up and coughed and sat in his underwear hacking and scratching before he would get up and go to the door and open it to spit outside.

It was still dark.

"Wake up, boy," Gustaf said. "We have to go make coffee and get to work."

The boy rolled out of bed and slipped his shoes on and followed Gustaf outside where he tried to cough and scratch and act like the men though it didn't seem to work very well.

They went to the cook trailer to make coffee and when it was boiled in the big pot on the stove Gustaf made some biscuits that everybody complained about even though they ate them all; the boy saw one man cleaning up the crumbs with the edge of his hand and eating from his cupped palm.

Then they went to work. All that morning the boy rode in a truck with the man named Pete. He had hands as big as one of the burners on the wood stove in the cook trailer and chewed snoose that he spit all the time.

Sometimes he would spit out the window and sometimes he would spit on the floor of the truck and sometimes he would spit on the dashboard of the truck. It looked to the boy as if he had been spitting on the dashboard for a long time because the buildup of dried and sticky tobacco juice was over an inch thick.

Pete's continuous spitting looked like fun and so the boy tried it, spitting first out the window, then on the floor and the dashboard, and he would have spent the whole day spitting and spitting, but soon he ran out of it because he did not have snoose to make more.

And still there was the whole day left. The boy became bored, finally, and the day seemed to drag until he thought he'd never been anywhere but in the truck—was born in the truck and lived in the truck. He made a whole game of being in the truck and because he missed his mother he thought of how it would be to live in a truck with his mother so that it would be a home.

There could be curtains over the windows and a small table with small chairs and a small radio where he and a small Clara could listen to the radio but they wouldn't allow a small Casey. . . .

He missed his mother.

And in the end, sitting that long day in the truck when all his spit was gone, in the end he missed his mother so that he could hardly stand it.

At last the day was done and all the men came back to the cook trailer. The boy helped Gustaf to make another pot of stew, and it only bothered him a little that they didn't clean the pot from the night before.

He ate with them and helped to clear the tables and sat in Gustaf's lap while the men played cards and slapped the cards down and laughed and swore.

But he had seen the cards before and watched them play before and seen the inside of the cook trailer before and he couldn't be excited by it anymore.

And he missed his mother.

Sitting there in Gustaf's lap he wanted to cry, and before he could stop it he was crying, which embarrassed him because the men could see him cry.

"What's the matter?" Gustaf asked.

"I miss my mother," he said. "I miss my mother and I want to go home...." The crying grew worse and he wanted to swear at himself for crying in front of the men because it embarrassed him, but he didn't yet know how the words worked for swearing.

"Dirty damn," he said, but it just made the feeling worse, and he grew sadder and cried harder until he was gulping with it.

All the men thought they could cheer him up, and they tried making faces and tickling him and laughing and holding him, but it still only seemed to get worse.

He could not stop crying, and finally he just sat in Gustaf's lap and cried and cried until the tears wore out.

Then he sniffled and sipped some warm milk one of the men made for him, warm milk with sugar in it, and it didn't feel so bad. He still missed his mother and felt sad, but something came from all the men, all the big and dirty and smelly men—something warm and soft—and he finally fell asleep in Gustaf's arms again.

FOURTEEN

GUSTAF carried him to Harvey's bed in the men's sleeping trailer, but the boy was not so sound asleep that he couldn't hear them talking.

"Poor little guy," one of them said.

"It's this damn war," another said. "Women out working in the cities. Who ever heard of such a thing?"

"He should be with his mother—and never mind this other business."

"Poor little guy."

The boy wanted to tell them that it was

all right, that he didn't mind the war or living in the city, but they all went to bed without turning on the lights and he fell back to sleep.

In the morning when he opened his eyes his grandmother was there.

Like magic. He had been asleep in the men's trailer and when he awakened the men were gone and his grandmother was sitting on the edge of Harvey's bunk brushing the hair away from his eyes, smiling down on him.

"Good morning, little thimble," she said.

"Where is Harvey?" he asked.

"He had to go be in the hospital for a while so they can fix his arm."

"I learned all about spitting yesterday."

"Oh you did, did you?"

He nodded. "In the truck. We spit and spit until I couldn't make any more spit. I drove the truck again and played cards and then I cried."

"Why did you cry?"

"Because I miss Mother. I like to be with you and the men and the trucks, but I really miss Mother." Here he started to cry again and he bit his lip to make himself stop.

"Do you want to go home?" his grandmother asked.

He nodded. "Yes. I want to go home and be with Mother."

She smiled. "Well then, I have good news for you. When we took Harvey to the hospital I went to the telegraph office and sent a telegram to your mother."

"What's a telegram?"

"It's a way to talk over a wire."

"Like a telephone?"

She nodded. "Something like that except that the message comes in writing. Like a letter over the wire." She reached into her apron pocket. "And your mother sent a wire for you."

She unfolded a yellow piece of paper with wings across the top. "This is for you."

He took the paper. There were letters all over it, and words. He knew all the letters by heart but did not yet know how to make them into words.

"I can't read what she says. Would you read it to me?"

She took the paper back and read it to him, moving her finger along with the words as she read:

"Dear Pumpkin—"

"She calls me pumpkin," he said. "Sometimes. Do I look like a pumpkin?"

"You must stop talking or I can't read to you."

"I'm sorry."

"Dear Pumpkin,
Mama writes that you miss me and want to come home. I miss you too very much and want to see you.
So I'm sending you some money for a ticket and Mama will put you on the train and you can come back to Chicago.
I love you."

His grandmother put the yellow paper on the table and he looked at it and touched it with wonder.

So much in just some words on the yellow paper with the wings at the top. All about his mother and her loving him and wanting to see him and be with him and how he would ride on the train two nights again and see her and not miss her anymore—all on the paper. All of his life on the yellow paper there on the table in the cook trailer.

"I'm going home," he said to his grand-mother.

She nodded.

"When?"

"Not tomorrow but the next day."

And he thought of that and found his hand going out to her apron to hold it. "But I will miss you too."

She was crying now, but he smiled. "Why don't you come with me and we can all live together and I won't have to miss either one?"

But she shook her head. "No. There is a time for living apart and your mother has come to that time. She must have her own life."

None of this made sense to the boy, but she had such a tightness to her voice that he didn't say anything.

And the day passed while he played around the cook trailer and helped his grandmother set the table and feed the men.

There was nothing different and yet there was—something had changed. He seemed to be waiting and his grandmother seemed to be waiting and even the men seemed to be wait-ing, but the boy could not understand why except that he was to leave.

That night he had a piece of apple pie with

milk made from the can and mice came out and ran around the floors and the boy and his grandmother chased them with brooms and a flyswatter and they screamed and the boy laughed until he nearly peed in his pants.

Then they sat on the bed and his grandmother held him. She told him stories of what it was like when she was a small girl in the old country and later when she came over on the boat as a half-grown girl.

And her husband who became his grandfather, a man the boy never knew.

"Clarence," she said as she talked of him. "His name was Clarence and he had straight shoulders and could outwork three men." Her eyes had a light in them when she said his name.

She told of their small farm in the northern prairie and of animals they owned and how it was when his mother was born.

She told of all the times of her life, sitting there in the cook trailer, of all the sad times and happy times. Of her wedding and the death of her husband, his grandfather, of the farm when he was gone and how she had to sell it and go to work; told of how Clarence would sit in the evenings and play on a violin he had made himself from planed spruce boards; told of men who came to court her when he died and how she turned them all away; told of summer evenings and winter storms, of hot days and cold nights, of mountains in Norway and trees that were so big five men couldn't reach around them, and a meal she cooked, a single meal for over fifty men who came to thrash the grain on their farm; told of happiness and sorrow, of two children she had that died before they were three and were buried under wood markers in back of the house; told of nights and making candy in the kitchen on their farm and slaughtering hogs in the fall. Told of a touch, a single touch from her own mother that made her feel good when she had the fever, and a scream, a single scream that almost stopped her heart, from a woman whose baby had been killed by a horse; told of raking hay and smelling silage in the late summer when it was cut and chopped green and packed into the silo for winter; told of the beginning of all the boy would ever know and the end of many things he would never know.

And the boy listened.

Through a whole night he sat and listened

to each story though he did not understand most of them. He did not sleep but sat in her lap with his head against her arm and listened to each story, each part of her life and did not ask questions or break into her talk.

He listened and did not know why—listened until it was time to cook for the men and she put him under the covers and he did not know why he did not sleep, did not quit listening, did not feel tired. . . .

Did not know then that he would take the train with a new note on his jacket, take it back to Chicago to his mother and that Casey, Uncle Casey, would be gone or that the war would end in another year or that he would see his father who came back from Europe and go to live with his mother and father in many new places; in Texas and Washington and the Philippine Islands and California and New York, in all the places where the army told his father to live. . . .

In all the places where his grandmother did not live.

He did not know then that year and year and year would pass and all he would see of his grandmother would be Christmas cards once a year with flowers on them, cards that said she loved them, loved him, missed him.

But not her.

He would spend year on year living in all the places where his grandmother did not live and would not see her until he was tall and had a broken voice and could not ever again sit in her lap and lean against her arm and hear her tell of her life. Of all her life.

But he did not know that then, on that night, did not know that he would never see his grandmother again as a boy, as her little thimble.

So he listened to her and rode in the truck to the depot again. There he boarded the train where the same conductor sat him in a seat for the trip down to Minneapolis, there to change again and take another train to Chicago where his mother waited on the platform, the steam from the engine rising around her like gentle smoke.

She was crying and laughing at the same time, kneeling on the platform so he could let go of the conductor's hand and run into her arms.

"I drove a truck," he said when she picked

him up and hugged him. She made soft mother sounds in his ear.

"I drove a truck and a cat and helped to cook and clean the cook trailer and kill mice—and I missed you so much I cried."

And here she held him out so she could see him better and said:

"I missed you, too, Pumpkin. It's so good to see you."

And she started to cry again and the boy thought how much her face looked like his grandmother's face when she cried at the depot as she put him on the train.

Same face. The same cheekbones and eyes as she cried.

"You look just like Grandma when you cry," he said. "Just like her . . ."

And he had a moment of sadness, some cutting thing that went through him that he did not understand then and would not understand until he was much, much older. An intense feeling of missing something and he did not know even what it was. . . .

Then it was gone, the feeling, gone and gone, and his mother took his hand and he followed her out of the station and into his life.

PORTRAIT

SHE WAS born in a time and place when not many babies lived. Most of them died of fevers or infections. In back of her childhood house there were several graves surrounded by a low white fence, each grave marked by a wooden placard painted white with flowers in a pretty design around the edges.

She remembered the graves all her life. Remembered the nearness of death. Each name on each small placard stayed in her memory, and even when she was old they were her brothers and sisters, as much as the ones who lived.

Eleven children were born in her family. Six boys and five girls; four boys lived and only two girls.

When she was still barely to her father's waist the family left Norway and came to America, then traveled by old steam train to Minneapolis and north to the prairie on the edge of the northern woods by wagon and, finally, by walking.

It was 1904 and she was twelve years old. She was a slight girl, thin but strong, with large brown eyes and rich brown hair that hung down her back to her knees.

Her father's brother had a farm that he had carved from the woods, and her father hand-cleared forty acres nearby. This work took two years and he cleared another forty, which took another two, and during the clearing of the land, during those four years, she grew into womanhood and became so beautiful her father joked about having to carry a club to beat suitors away.

It perhaps was not quite that bad. But the young men *did* come in droves—some on foot from as far as fifty miles away—just to sit in front of the clapboard house her father made and tell her of their hopes, dreams. Or just to sit shyly and stare at the ground and be seen by her.

Clarence was such a young man. Painfully, almost hopelessly shy, he had walked thirty miles to introduce himself to her father and had then been unable to say anything to her but to stammer out his name and say:

"I am of the land. . . ."

And then sit in blank silence with his hands clasped in front of him staring at the ground.

And she loved him.

It came to her that way. Of all the suitors she did not just love him the best, think more of him—she did not compare him to others.

She loved him only, starting at once and for all the time they knew each other she loved him and only him and he loved her the same hard, intense, full way.

They were married by a Lutheran circuit minister, and Clarence wore a stiff black suit with a celluloid collar that made him look like he had a rail up his backside, and they posed for a man who had a wooden box camera nearly as large as a wagon: she in her beauty and youth and he looking somehow boiled and scrubbed. They paid a small amount extra to have the picture tinted so there is light skin tone and a blush to their cheeks, and for their life together and for hers later after he died—for all of that they kept the picture on the wall.

They built a farm where a river flowed into a small lake. First a small house, then the barn and granary and smokehouse for smoking meat, and she set about the business of having a family.

She bore nine children—one every other year for eighteen years—and remained beautiful in spite of it. Or perhaps because of it.

Seven of the children lived to maturity whereupon one son was taken into the army, trained briefly, and then blown to pieces on an island in the Pacific by a defective artillery round he was trying to load. A daughter was killed in a car accident while driving drunk and the rest of the children including the boy's mother married, had children, some remarried and had more children, then died, all of them of heart trouble or cancer or living, and she outlived them all. She outlived all her children, but somehow was not destroyed by it, accepted their ends as she finally did her own.

Through it all, through ninety-two years, she never lost her joy or her beauty or her gladness at living, at seeing each new day; never lost the feeling of celebration at seeing her grandchildren, and when the one who had been the little thimble, who hid from the men in back of her apron, when he came to visit as a grown man and had children to show her, she took his small son into the kitchen and sat him down and stole him completely and utterly with one piece of apple pie and a glass of milk.

"See," the new boy said to his father. "There is sugar and simmanon on top. . . ."

And she looked up and smiled at him, a smile that cut across all the years and made him wish he could sit in her lap—an intense, cutting longing.

"Would you like some pie?" she asked.

And of course he did and he sat and ate the pie and drank the milk and wished to God that all good things could go on forever and ever.

GARY PAULSEN is one of the most distinguished and best-loved writers of young adult literature today. Three of his novels — *Hatchet, Dogsong,* and *The Winter Room* — were Newbery Honor Books. His books frequently appear on the best books lists of the American Library Association.

Born May 17, 1939, he developed a passion for reading and a love of adventure at an early age. He has worked on a farm and as an engineer, construction worker, ranch hand, truck driver and sailor, as well as competing twice in the 1,180-mile Alaskan dogsled race, the Iditarod. Many of these experiences have found their way into his books.

Paulsen and his wife, Ruth Wright Paulsen, an artist who has illustrated several of his books, divide their time between a home in New Mexico and a boat in the Pacific.

Something for Everyone

Step into unknown realms, or travel around the United States. Read about times long gone, or step into the future. Laugh at light-hearted revenge, or cry along as entire towns suffer oppressive times. Take a break from your everyday and explore a new place — it's reading like never before.

 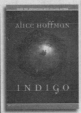    

Available wherever you buy books, or use this order form!

- ❏ 0-439-36786-7 Bluish by Virginia Hamilton $4.99 US
- ❏ 0-439-05948-8 Adaline Falling Star by Mary Pope Osborne $4.99 US
- ❏ 0-439-47220-2 Spellfall by Katherine Roberts $5.99
- ❏ 0-439-26327-1 The Seeing Stone by Kevin Crossley-Holland $6.99 US
- ❏ 0-439-22420-9 The Firework-Maker's Daughter by Philip Pullman $4.99 US
- ❏ 0-439-27200-9 Witness by Karen Hesse $5.99

- ❏ 0-439-10838-1 The Unicorn Chronicles #1: Into the Land of the Unicorns by Bruce Coville $4.50 US
- ❏ 0-439-24219-3 Midnight Magic by Avi $4.99 US
- ❏ 0-439-19314-1 Blister by Susan Shreve $4.99 US
- ❏ 0-439-52357-5 The Cookcamp by Gary Paulsen $4.99 US
- ❏ 0-590-69222-4 United Tates of America by Paula Danziger $5.99 US
- ❏ 0-439-25636-4 Indigo by Alice Hoffman $4.99 US

Scholastic Inc., P.O. Box 7502, Jefferson City, MO 65102

Please send me the books I have checked above. I am enclosing $_____ (please add $2.00 to cover shipping and handling). Send check or money order-no cash or C.O.D.s please.

Name _____ Birth Date _____

Address _____

City _____ State/ZIP _____

Please allow four to six weeks for delivery. Offer good in U.S.A. only. Sorry, mail orders are not available to residents of Canada. Prices subject to change.

■ SCHOLASTIC   www.scholastic.com   SIGN60